FIVE
LITTLE
FIREMEN

by MARGARET WISE BROWN
and EDITH THACHER HURD

PICTURES BY TIBOR GERGELY

SIMON AND SCHUSTER · NEW YORK

THE LITTLE GOLDEN BOOKS ARE PREPARED
UNDER THE SUPERVISION OF
MARY REED, Ph.D.
FORMERLY OF TEACHERS COLLEGE,
COLUMBIA UNIVERSITY

Authors and Artist

This is the first Golden Book on which
Margaret Wise Brown and Edith
Thacher Hurd, both writers of many
distinguished books for children, have
collaborated.
Tibor Gergely has illustrated many of
the Little Golden Books, including
THE TAXI THAT HURRIED and TOOTLE.

A LITTLE HOUSE caught on fire.

The fire started so quietly, and it was such a little fire at first.

A flame like a little mouse came darting in and out of a hole in the hall closet and darted back again. A policeman smelled it.

But it grew and sizzled, and the house began to smoke, and the smoke blew out the window.

And then the policeman saw it. He peeked in the cellar window and saw the yellow flames in the gray smoke.

So he ran to the corner, opened the red alarm box, and called the Fire Department. Then he went back to the house.

Ding, ding, ding,
Rings the fire alarm in the little fire station.
Ding, ding, ding—
Five little firemen slide down the firehouse
pole.

"Sparks!" shouts the First Little Fireman.

He puts on his white helmet, twirls his black mustache, and jumps into the little red Chief's car with its shiny brass bell. Cling, clang!

The First Little Fireman has to be the first at the fire, to tell all the other firemen what to do when they get there.

He is the fire chief.

"A fire won't wait," says the Second Little Fireman. Round as a pumpkin, he jumps into the driver's seat of the hook-and-ladder truck, the biggest fire engine of all.

"We'll save all the people," says the Third Little Fireman.

The Third Little Fireman jumps on the
side of the hook-and-ladder truck as it rolls
out the door. He has muscles as big as
baseballs, he is that strong. He runs up the
ladders and carries the people down the
ladders—that Third Little Fireman.

"We'll squirt lots of water," says the Fourth Little Fireman, who is bright as a button and so drives the huge tower truck.

"I sneeze in the smoke," says the Fifth Little Fireman. Spry as a fly, he jumps on his hose truck and roars out the firehouse door.

With a Clang, cling, clang
and a Wheeeeeeeee
and a Whoooooooo
the tires of the trucks go hissing around,
leaving the firehouse behind.
Clang, cling, clang—
the Chief's bell.
Whee-ee, whee-ee, whee-ee—
the tower truck's siren.
Dong, dong, dong,
the hose truck skids around the corner.
Whooooooooooooooooooooooooooooooooo,
wails the long hook-and-ladder truck,
the biggest fire engine of them all.

Get out of the way!
Get out of the way!
Here come
the Five Little Firemen.
With a clang, cling, clang,
   and a Wheeeeeeee
      and a Whooooooooooooooooooooooooooooo
they go whizzing up a street called Oak Street

then whizzing
around a corner
into 12½ Street

down Asphalt Avenue

then down Eucalyptus Drive

and up the King's Highway

and over Baseball Boulevard

to Small Bush Road.
Dong, dong, dong

And there on Small Bush Road was the little house on fire.

Flames the size of pocket handkerchiefs were waving out of the windows. And lots of smoke!

When the policeman got to the door, the
door was on fire.

"Chop it down," he ordered.

But he kicked it down with his foot and ran
upstairs and woke up a very sleepy family,

who all started sneezing with the smoke.

This was the Hurricane Jones Family, and they were terribly sleepy.

"Grab what you love most and run out of your house," ordered the policeman.

Mrs. Hurricane Jones tried to grab her three little boys and run out of the house with them; but when she went to grab them, the first little boy had run to grab his cat, the second little boy had run downstairs and out of the house to take care of his rabbits, and the third little boy had grabbed all the flowers that he had picked the day before and was halfway down the stairs with them.

So Mrs. Hurricane Jones, still very sleepy, threw her mirrors out the window and picked up her pillow and ran downstairs.

Mr. Hurricane Jones grabbed his pipe and his matches and came afterwards to be sure that all his family were out of the house and standing in a line on the lawn.

And there they were, all safely out on their front lawn, each holding in his arms what he loved most, when the firemen came along.

But where is the Hurricane Jones's jolly fat cook?

The Five Little Firemen, brave as can be, get to work.

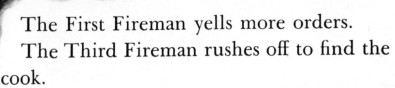

The First Fireman yells more orders.

The Third Fireman rushes off to find the cook.

The Second Fireman backs the hook-and-ladder truck into just the right place. The Hurricane Jones's house is too tiny for big ladders. So he takes one of the little ladders and puts it up to the side of the house.

The Fourth Little Fireman points the water tower at the flames and squirts.

And the Fifth Little Fireman unrolls the hose and screws it onto the red fire hydrant.

He turns it on and water that runs under the streets in big pipes all the time rushes through the hose.

Sh-sh-sh it squirts out of the nozzle like a roaring river through the air.

Swishhsh—they smash in the windows to let out the smoke.

And swishhsh—in roars the water to put out the flames.

The smoke gets all brown and yellow when the water hits it.

They chop down the burning wood and throw fireproof blankets over the furniture.

The Third Little Fireman has found the cook and he wants to carry her down the ladder on his back in the fireman's carry. "Nix," says she.

She is too fat to carry and too big to jump into a net and too jolly to stay and burn up in the flames.

So they shoot up the life-line for the Hurricane Jones's jolly fat cook to slide down.

And down she comes.

"Jewallopers!" says she. "It was getting warm up there."

And soon all the bright flames were wet black ashes and the crackling sound of the flames was quiet and there was only the great purring of the red hose truck pumping water and the bright searchlights of the fire engines

making the trees and the bushes much greener than they had been before. The fire was over, and the Hurricane Jones Family went home with their Uncle Clement to sleep and to wait for their house to be fixed.

"Fire's out," calls the Chief, and that First Little Fireman climbs into his shiny red car.

"Let's go," says the Second Little Fireman.

"That was some cook," says the Third Little Fireman.

"Some fire!" says the Fourth Little Fireman.

"Kerchew," says the Fifth Little Fireman, as he rolls in his hose.

Then the engines back up, turn around, roar, and go away.

Only their bells clang slowly now,
Clang, Cling, Clong,

and a ding, ding, ding,
they all go back to the firehouse.

The Five Little Firemen have black on their faces and black on their hands. The Chief's mustache is blacker than ever.

Their rubber coats and helmets are shiny wet with water from the hose.

The Five Little Firemen are tired.

"That's that," says the First Little Fireman.
"Whow," says the Second Little Fireman.
"Whee," says the Third Little Fireman.
"Whew," says the Fourth Little Fireman.
"Home!" says the Fifth Little Fireman.
. They have to wash the fire engines. Then they polish the bells and the sirens and all their equipment to be ready for another fire alarm at any minute, should one come.

At last the Five Little Firemen hang up
their helmets and black rubber coats. They
wash their hands and faces.

There is no other fire alarm that night.

So the Five Little Firemen sit down to
supper and sing songs and laugh and eat a
lot of Irish stew.

There never are many fires. That is why
the Five Little Firemen are so fat—all but
one.

Five Sleepy Firemen jump into bed.
Five Little Firemen,
Brave as can be,
Sleep, and they dream
Of the beautiful sea.

THE FIREMEN'S DREAM

Flames and smoke
And the glass that broke
And the fires that rise
Into the skies
And scorch the stars
And motor cars
That hurry along
When they hear the gong
And the Wh o o o o
And the Wh e e e e e
And the ding, ding, dong—
These are all things
To sing about.

"O yes, O no.
There is no doubt,
The finest fire
Is the fire that's out.
Good night."

G